Alexander R. Eagar

Prometheus

And other Poems

Alexander R. Eagar

Prometheus
And other Poems

ISBN/EAN: 9783744772808

Printed in Europe, USA, Canada, Australia, Japan

Cover: Foto ©Andreas Hilbeck / pixelio.de

More available books at **www.hansebooks.com**

PROMETHEUS,

AND OTHER POEMS.

BY

ALEXANDER R. EAGAR,

B. A., T. C. D.

DUBLIN:

E. PONSONBY, 116, GRAFTON-STREET.

LONDON: SIMPKIN, MARSHALL, & Co.

1877.

TO

MY FATHER AND MOTHER

I dedicate

THESE SONGS OF IDLE HOURS.

Contents.

CONTENTS.

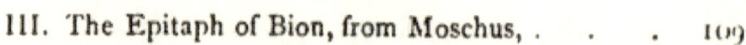

TRANSLATIONS FROM THE GREEK:

    I. From the Bacchæ of Euripides, ... 101

    II. From the Hecuba of Euripides, ... 106

    III. The Epitaph of Bion, from Moschus, . . . 109

"It is not only the eagle of Zeus that bathes in Helicon, nor is it only the winged steed of the Muses that drinks of its water. The swallows dip their wings therein, and even the very flies taste the sweet stream. They do but sip, it is true; but do they not sip of Helicon?"

Prometheus.

HIGH in the sombre stillness of the air,—
 Where strong-beaked eagles flap their dusky wings,
 And the unjoying wailing tempest sings ;
Where Caucasus exalts his summit bare,—
Stands a lone altar, strewn with bones ; and there
 The children of the earth were wont to meet,
 To pour their riches at the royal feet
Of Zeus, the god who loves his children's care,—
Of Zeus, the god who loves not giftless prayer.

Here men would meet, what time the new-born day
 Poured a bleak brightness on the altar-stone :
 And then went up to heaven the dying moan
Of the struck steer, trembling beneath the ray
That lit the sacred knife upraised to slay.
 And now his lustrous eyes are glazed with death,
 And the pleased gods send down the living breath
Of air to fan the flickering flames that play
Around the sacrifice, as fierce as they.

B

Here by the stone the son of Japet stood,
  With wild eyes looking to the burning dawn ;
  His shaggy eye-brows o'er his eyes down-drawn ;
His hair enridged and waving, like the flood
Of the dark Euxine, when the tempests hood
  The heights of Heaven ; and his squarèd brow
  Was smooth as crystal,—not with peace—for now
His swollen veins are marks of angry mood,
In the quick throbbings of the boiling blood.

" O Zeus," he cries, " O faithless and untrue,
  Perjured and weak one, is it but for nought
  That we have lives in rich oblation brought
To thee and all thy brother gods ? while you,
Helpless to aid us and unwilling, view
  Us toiling on this earth, which is a hell,
  For bootless profit and for pleasures fell ;
Ye helpless heartless ones,—a fitter crew
To pray to us, than we from you to sue !

" O mighty Zeus, to thee are paid the lives
  Of unoffending kids and fleecy lambs,
  And bearded he-goats and unyielding rams ;
For thee the young bull at the altar strives,
And his unequal bonds in sunder rives ;

For thee he dies ; but thou canst not restore,
To him or to his giver, life once more,
When once his victims ruthless Hermes drives
To death, and Hades binds them in his gyves.

" Unpitying one, I saw, but yesterday,
A maiden led to yield to thee her breath ;
She closed her eyes to open them on death ;—
Say, does the King of Life and Death obey
Thy cruel orders, Lord of Heaven ? say
Canst thou restore that maiden's life again ?
Thou canst not, Zeus! Then why, with labour-
pain,
Should we, to please thee, tread a thorny way,
To reach sad Nothingness's border grey ?

"Ah me! but yesterday I saw her lie,
White on the dusky marble ; robe and veil
Torn from her lithe light limbs ; and from her pale
Sad face dark hopeless eyes looked up on high,
Glancing a brief last glance upon the sky ;
And thou didst cover the blue sky with grey
And lightless mantlings of the clouds, that they
Might hide Heaven's beauty from the maiden's eye ;—
The maiden doomed to look but once, and die.

"Ah me! I saw her naked white limbs shrink
   From the cold marble, and her wind-wooed hair
   Stirred with the slayer's breath ; and in her bare
Soft breast I saw his cruel fingers sink :
And her bright curls, which lay in many a link
   Of gold across the marble road of life,
   Were torn aside by thine accursèd knife :
I saw no more, till, on the altar-brink,
I saw the snows her yielded life-blood drink.

"I saw no more ; and yet I seemed to see
   Thee, sitting with the gods in thy high Heaven,
   Playing with circlings of the planets seven,
Great cruel children ; and ye laughed at me,
And at my brethren of the earth, that we
   (Still weaker children) paid you with the flower
   Of rosy blood of girls and boys, each hour,
For gifts not given us by your decree ;—
For gifts unheld, unsent, by such as ye."

But Zeus is Lord of Death and King of Pain,
And curbed his foe with vulture and with chain.

A Death Song.

GIVE me the cup,
And brim it with crimson wine !
  Fill, friend, fill it up
With the richest draught of the Rhine !
  Let the beaded ripples flow,
  And the liquid rubies glow
On the wave divine.
  This is the draught for me,
  And my burning spirits crave it :
  By the warm soft waves of a southern sea
  Grew the purple fruit that gave it.
The seed was warmed in the bosom fair
Of a laughing maiden, whose golden hair
  Was wreathed with such leaves as crown the bowl ;
And the white sun filled all the liquor rare
  With a soul.

And the vines of that vineyard above the rest
Were purple and heavy; but one was best,
And of all its clusters full and fair
The richest was sought for my goblet there.
It was plucked by a maid from the drooping vine;
And now it is with us!   Then pour the wine,
Till I taste of the soul of the sunny Rhine,
And live in its life; for death is nigh;
I must sing one song before I die.

See, how the goblet is brimming o'er,
    And the ripples are leaping to greet the light!
Leap!   When ye saw the day before,
    The crone that is shading her fading sight
From the light ye love, was a leaping child,
And her laughter wild
Was sweet as the songs of the maidens three,
Whose soft white limbs, to the supple knee,
Were red as they pressed this wine for me.
Leap! for the days of their song are o'er,
And ye shall be seen in the light no more,
And I shall be still as you or they,
Ere the hills are dyed with the dawn of day.

Strike the lyre for me !
And oh, for a harp of a thousand strings
To swell with the strain that my spirit sings !—
    A strain that is meet with such wine to be.
As a hundred suns and a hundred showers,
And a hundred odours of Rhineland flowers,
    Were given to ripen this cup of wine ;
So many a joy and many a pain,
And many an all but perfect strain,
    Were given to swell in this song of mine.
Deep in the bass must there ever be
The low sweet sound of the saddened sea,
    And the piercing wail of the sweeping wind :—
And over it all must the triumph swell
Of the song that was heard, as poets tell,
When Bacchanals tasted the storèd bliss
Of a wine that was less divine than this.
    The notes of triumph thrill my mind ;
And I long for the sound of striving men
And singing maidens to rise again
O'er the sea's deep bass ;—for a strain of the sea
Alone is meet with such wine to be.

Before I die
I must sing one song :—what shall it be,
To be meet to chime with the strain of the sea,
    To be sung when such wine is nigh ?
A song of round limbs gleaming bare
With opal light, and of yellow hair
Wreathèd with purple clusters fair ?
A song of the Thracian mountain-crests,
And of Bacchanals staining their snow-white breasts
With the crimson blood of the fruit divine ?
A song of the mighty god of wine,
Pouring his gifts on the plain for men ?
Nay—I shall sing not of him again !
This goblet is better than his could be·:—
Then what is god Bacchus to thee or me ?

Nay, I shall sing of one I know !
For her alone do the rubies glow
In the light-sought deeps of this cup of wine,
And for her alone is this song of mine.
I shall sing my song to the rose below ;
And the breezes that rich with its sweetness blow

Shall carry my song o'er the hills away,
Till the time when their brows are red with day.
They shall blow on her cheek and her forehead fair,
And then they shall leave in her gleaming hair
The scent of my song and the rose;—when I
Have passed away as the rose-leaves die.
And the morning star, that is looking down
On the purple sheen of my goblet's crown,
Shall gleam with one wine-red ray, as he dies,
On the morn-grey light of her opening eyes.
This is the song that is meet to be
Sung with the strain of the deathless sea;
This is the song that, in death divine,
I shall sing, with a cup of this peerless wine!

Doubt.

I KNOW, O Lord, that I am small to thee ;
   That very weak my strongest faith appears ;
   That very feeble are my doubts and fears ;
But these weak fears, O God, are strong in me.
I am not gifted with the strength I see,—
   For this I thank thee, Lord,—in him who sears
   My doubt-sore soul with bitter words, or sneers,
Or thanks that all his creeds untroubled be.
I look into my soul, my Lord, and there
   I only trust the clearness of thine eye
Viewing the darkening floods, where not the glare
   Of all earth's noons can show the deeps that lie.
Is there no time when all the waves are fair,
   Save in the shallow seas that glass the sky?

Sin.

WILT thou reject me, Lord, for that one stain
   Which fell upon the mirror of my soul ?
   Must it destroy the brightness of the whole ?
Wilt thou deny the wholesome latter rain
For but one tare amid the thriving grain ?
   See, Lord, but one blot dyes the snowy roll ;
   But one small rent is in the silken stole ;
Wilt thou not wear it, then, when thou dost reign ?
Alas ! the blight is on me, and my heart
   May not by knife or burning savèd be.
The spotted peach, for which the gardener's art
   Is bootless, speaks to me, " My brother, we
Have both slow rotted from one poisoned part :—
   And shall God break His laws to humour thee ? "

"Sursum Corda."

I SEE the triple mountain capped with snow ;
   Above the clouds the peaks to Heaven rise,
   The silver-shining summits kiss the skies,
And, lost in glory, spurn the earth below.
The sunlight clothes them in a golden glow,
   While, o'er the lake, the gliding Zephyr sighs;
   Below, the earth in all its beauty lies ;
Above, the grey clouds float and breezes blow.
E'en so, my heart, despising all that bears
   The taint of earth, mount up, nor linger here :
One soul is godlike,—that which ne'er despairs
   To gain the height of heights, devoid of fear :
The grandest point on earth the spirit dares
   Is but a step to reach a higher sphere.

MAC GILLYCUDDY'S REEKS,
   March, 1874.

Sarsfield and Walker.

ERE the moon fled before the morning hours,
  My spirit flew to that ecstatic shore
  Where heroes who have passed, their warfare o'er,
Lead a new life in unimagined bowers;
And there two walked among unfading flowers,
  This clad in mail, and that a cassock wore:
  One fought at Limerick, till the streets ran gore,
The other held fair Derry's maiden towers.
I wondering asked them why with linkèd hands
  They roamed together; and a halo shed
    Its light around at their serene reply:
"Since our weak earthly bodies died, the bands
  Of misty form, that severed us, are dead;
    But love and truth, which join us, do not die."

Sonnet.

O MAIDEN mine, though loving were a sin,
　　Though each fond word were black as murder's
　　　　stain,
　　Though each kind deed were as the sin of Cain,
Still, if I hoped thy gentle heart to win,
My soul, untaught before, would then begin
　　To worship at love's shrine ; my busy brain
　　Would still invent some mode in which to gain
Thy better love than that of kith or kin.
And then, perchance, thou would'st believe that I
　　Did love thee with a love surpassing love ;
But now, when loving is no sinning, why
　　Will not thy heart to mine responsive move ?
Thou wilt not even love me ; I would die,
　　If by my death my loving I could prove.

Sonnet.

THE soldier, captive mid a foreign band,
 Desires to see his country's flag once more;
 The sailor, wrecked upon a barren shore,
Paces the brown and sultry desert strand,
And looks out o'er the waste of wave-wet sand,
 And o'er the waves (which ever rise and roar
 With the same restless passion as of yore),
Longing to see again his motherland.
So I, my darling, when from thee apart
 Amid the city's thousand joys and cares,
Felt a warm constant longing fill my heart
  To see again the depths of those grey eyes,
  Whose lightest love-glance was a worthy prize
For all my work, a goal for all my prayers.

The Song of the Skylark.

DEDICATION.

I WATCHED the little lark rise up from earth,
  And pour his glad notes from his panting breast,
  Singing the song of all sweet songs the best,
The song that tells the beauty of the birth
Of Love,—fair king of sorrow and of mirth.
  And, as he sang, he hovered o'er his nest,
  As watching for his loved one's least behest.
What his song said, I knew ; and felt the dearth
Of words to tell the glorious mystery
    That filled my heart ; but as I mused, thine eyes
    Shone on my soul, and it burst forth in song
That blended with the lark's pure melody :—
    So my soul sang to thine, amid the strong
  Sweet music of the bird that knows the skies.

The Song of the Skylark.

Up! Up! Up!
To the realms of the Sun and Moon!
Up! Up! Up!
To the eyes of golden-haired Noon!
With song welling forth like wine from the cup,
The Skylark soars on earth-scorning wings,
Singing a song all of heavenly things;
And this is the strain of the song that he sings.

" Leaving earth below,—
Earth, all toil and sorrow,—
To the land I go
Of a glad to-morrow.
Fairer than the snow
On the hills at morning!—
Brighter than the glow
Evening's sky adorning!—

c

Better than the best
   Of the bright stars seven !—
Dearer than the rest
   Brought by dewy even !—
Loved-one of my breast !
   Rise with me to Heaven !

" Darling, I can see
   Earth and wave below me ;—
White ships riding free
   On the billows foamy ;
White waves leap to greet
   Rippling inland fountains ;
White clouds drop to meet
   Purple-crested mountains.
Cliff and rock and sea,
   All are fair as morning ;
All are but, to me,
   Gems thy crown adorning.
Love, I sing to thee,
   All earth's beauties scorning.

" Come, my darling, come !
   Leave the earth behind thee ;

Leave thy ground-built home ;
  Leave the ties that bind thee ;
Leave the toil of earth ;
  Leave its care and sorrow ;
This will be our birth
  To a glad to-morrow !
Come to me ; we'll fly
  Where the stars are shining,
To the lands that lie
  Past the sun's declining,
To the fields on high
  Bright as gold's refining.

" Come with me, my love ;
  Fly from earth to Heaven,—
To the home above
  Of the sweet stars seven.
Wilt thou not ?   Then down,
  Down from Heaven I hover;
To thy bosom brown
  Drops thy panting lover.
In thy humble nest
  Near the drooping willow.

Safely I will rest
Listening to the billow,
While thy heaving breast
Is my head's soft pillow."

The Wave.

THE Billows were tossing in fierce commotion,
   Clasping the careless Air,
When a young Wave rose from the depths of Ocean.
   The home of her sisters fair:
The wild Wind wooed her fiercely
   From the moment of her birth,
But he never could taste the longed-for bliss,
For she fled from his hated, chilling kiss,—
   She fled to the heartless Earth.

But the arrow-peaked rocks were cruel pillows
   For the head of the gentle Wave ;
And Earth cast her back among the billows,—
   He cast her back to her grave.
Before she sank in the Ocean,
   She leaped once more to his breast :
"O love, there is bliss in a death like this ;
I die on thy bosom !" One last short kiss,
   And she sank to eternal rest.

In Memoriam.

U. G. E.

Obiit March 17th, 1877.

A BRIGHT one spake to me, "Cease from thy tears ;
　They will not draw thy darling back again ;—
They will not give to gladden thy sad ears
　　Her loving voice ; or bring to ease thy pain
　　Her hand's soft touches ;—why dost thou complain
With fruitless weeping and with idle sorrow ?
Forget thy grief to-day, and smile to-morrow."

My heart made answer, ere my lips could speak :—
　" Unearthly one, thou know'st not death or birth ;
Thou hast not dwelt with us ; and dost thou seek
　　To still the weeping of a child of earth ?
　　I do not envy thine unthinking mirth :
But get thee hence, and learn what sorrows be,
And then, when thou hast wept, come comfort me."

I weep because our darling lately died
   In this sweet month of yellow daffodils,
When the green trees have donned their tufted pride,
   And the slight willows bend to kiss the rills,
   And the gay robin his pure love-song trills ;—
When all began to feel the holy breath
Of living spring, our darling tasted death.

I see the early violets droop and die ;
   They fall in youth, the children of a day ;
But all together on the cold earth lie ;
   Some do not live, while others pass away.
   Our darling died with no such fate as they ;
In the soft spring-time's fair and sunny hours,
Alone she fell among her sister flowers.

I weep because the clinging woodbine fades,
   And the pale daisy dies, but for the year :—
I weep because the comely woodland maids
   Gather fresh roses ere the leaves are sere :—
   And the slight violets shall again appear.
But when sweet spring brings back the cooing dove,
Thou shalt return to me no more, my love !

The robin sings as sang he yester-eve ;
  The crocus blooms as bloomed it yester-morn ;
The swaying oaks and beeches do not grieve ;
  The stars look down unchanged and not forlorn ;
  Perchance the spirits view my tears with scorn :—
But I am not a spirit or a tree,
But a still loving heart that weeps for thee.

I watch the young moon floating in the sky,
  A silver boat in golden-isled seas ;
Her silent-gliding prow is passing by
  The gleaming shores of the sweet Pleiades ;—
  God send the beauteous boat a guiding breeze !
For I am sure that it is bearing thee
To my bright heaven-isle to wait for me.

To my sweet heaven-isle where all is bright,
  And true friends meet there, never more to part ;
Men call it Sirius ;—and the guardian sprite
  Sends his soft light into my inmost heart :
  I know that there shall end all pain and smart :
And gazing on it oft, I long to be,
My loved-one, in that happy home with thee.

For here the earth is loveless, and the sea,
  Unmindful of thee, swells with joyous waves ;
But they, my best-loved friends, are laid with thee,
  Forgotten by the world, in lonely graves.
  On earth, we are but time's and chance's slaves.
Then let me dry my tears and hide my sorrow,
In the sweet longing for a glad to-morrow

𝔐emories.

I.

Pɪɴᴋ blossoms of woodbine seared with age,
  And a leaf of ivy dried and sere ;
Their life-blood is staining the yellow page
  Of a book unopened for many a year :

They were plucked in the glen when we walked alone :
  And your arms were filled with the wild red rose,
And the ferns I tore from the stream-bathed stone,
  And guelder-rose shedding its heapèd snows.

II.

My darling, my lost one, I seem to forget thee,
  As earth hath forgotten thee, long, long, ago :
The woods are as wild as the day that I met thee ;
  The hills are as bright in their mantles of snow :

But these are the woods and the hills far away, dear,
  From where I first met thee ;—they knew not the
    dead :
And I feel that the trees which remember that day,
    dear,
  Are watching in vain for the sound of thy tread.

Are watching in vain, dear, and vainly are weeping,
  And blossoms are peeping in vain through the
    grass,
By the brown-bouldered banks where soft Caragh is
    sleeping,
  To waken, my darling, no more as we pass.

I never can know ;—but I feel they regret thee :—
  I bade them farewell, darling, long, long, ago :
And I, with the earth, even seem to forget thee ;
  But hast thou forgotten ? I never can know.

III.

I have sinned, and hidden
  The secret in my breast :
It hath sprung unbidden
  Forth, to haunt my rest.

I have sinned, and weeping
  Cried in bitter pain,
While I waked ; and, sleeping,
  Waked to weep again.

Thou art ever near me ;
  Thou my sin hast known ;
But, my darling, hear me !
  Leave me not alone !

Something thou canst see, dear,
  Deeper far within ;
'Tis my love for thee, dear ;
  Guard me from my sin !

" 𝕎e Sing not the Songs of Old."

THEY sang of all things;—songs for joy and sorrow,
  And songs for small and great, for old and young,
And songs for feast to-night, for joust to-morrow;
  No hero's bier or bridal was unsung.

They sang of all things;—children in the meadows
  Playing 'mid daisies' silver, cowslips' gold;
Men toiling in the autumn's sun-red shadows;
  And tranquil rest and quiet for the old.

To-day they sang the war-song, 'mid the rattle
  Of pagan arrows by wild eastern seas;
To-morrow sang the praise of rest from battle,
  In arbours slumb'rous with the hum of bees.

The music of wild birds in greenwood singing
  Spake to the minstrels, "Brothers, bear your par‘
In praise with us;" the bells at sweet eve ringing
  Blended with solemn music in each heart.

They sang to all things ;—to the ship spice-laden,
　　The bird swift-flying to the waiting nest,
The youth war-willing, and the spinning maiden,
　　The babe soft-sleeping on the milk-white breast.

And all things living,—flowers that sleep at even,
　　Sweet-laden bees, and sweeter-burdened men,
Maids on low earth, and angels in high heaven,
　　Joined in the chorus with the minstrels then.

But we have learned to sing of deeper wonders
　　Than those which spring from glad earth's living
　　　　breath ;
With bared breast facing heaven's awful thunders,
　　Our minstrels ever sing that life is death.

We feel his shadow fill the air around us ;
　　We see it falling ever o'er our sight ;
We know that at our birth that shadow found us,
　　And, ever since, hath watched us day and night.

And day and night we sing the same dread story
　　Of death, in joy and sorrow, peace and strife.
But shall we ever share the final glory
　　Of those who saw and sang that life is life ?

They sang of all ;—the great and small together ;
  Seizing the weakest ray amid the dark,
Like diamonds that gleam in blackest weather,
  Or flash to glory 'neath one flinty spark.

To a Friend.

I.

You live in the creed that your mother taught you,
　　Without a doubt and without a fear;
And, trusting the love of Him Who bought you,
　　To your Father's God your soul draws near:

Like a ship that sails on a stormless ocean,
　　Leaving behind a barren strand,
And breeze-borne glides with an equal motion
　　To the shore of a distant lovely land.

And I know that you thank the mighty Father,
　　Who sends that breeze from His home above,
And guides you, safe from the storms that gather,
　　To rest in the haven of His love.

II.

But not for all is that peaceful sailing;
    Not for all does that fair breeze flow;
And the toil of the bravest is unavailing
    To guide their barks in the storms that blow.

Darkness above and about and before them,
    And wild waves surging around the sides,
And the might of the lowering tempest o'er them,
    And the wine-dark clouds that the lightning rides:

No sign in the storm of a star to guide them;
    The rocks are rising upon the lee:
Though the beacon-lights may beam beside them,
    In the heavy darkness they cannot see.

But when night is gone, and the day is nearing,
    They see the land o'er the curling wave,
And their friends of old on the shore appearing
    To welcome among them the true and brave.

D

But what of those who have bravely striven
  With heroes' spirit and giants' might,
To whom the strength has not been given
  To pierce the gloom of that awful night ?

Though many a ship the Lord doth cherish,
  And keep in the hollow of His hand,
How many a well-manned bark doth perish
  Far from the shore of that lovely land !

Why does not God in the night defend them
  From tempest's fury and surging wave ?
Why does not God in safety send them
  To the haven made for the true and brave ?

We know not why : but the Lord, Who gave them
  The storm and darkness to blind them here,
E'en at that fearful hour may save them
  'Mid blackened clouds and the tempest drear.

For He knows the dangers that environ ;
  He sees how the frail ships toss and reel ;
Will ye bind His Mercy with bands of iron ?
  Will ye curb His Strength with chains of steel ?

𝔄 ma 𝔆𝔥ère.

WHEN the lamps of the sky were lighted,
  And the moon shone bright above,
My spirit was roaming, benighted,
  Looking for her I love:

My body was wrapped in slumber,
  My eyelids closed from the light,
But my spirit, on ways without number,
  Was wandering out in the night.

" Whose is the name you are speaking ?
  Weary one, will you not tell
Who is the one you are seeking ?
  How may we know her well ?"

" I will whisper her name at even,
  Or breathe it at dawn of day;
And the planet that rules in heaven
  Shall carry my thoughts away,

To rest in her pure white bosom,
    And sleep on her eyes of light:
I will tell my thoughts to a blossom,
    And send it to her by night;

She shall taste of its fragrance, telling
    Of vows that are known above,
And her heart 'neath the flow'ret swelling
    Shall give to me all its love."

Then they laughed with light lips of scorning,
    And mockingly pointed at me;
And I wandered on till the morning,
    And woke without finding thee!

A Poet to his Mistress.

CLOSER to me, my darling; let thy loving hands
    clasp mine;
Look in my eyes, my darling, with those dove-soft
    eyes of thine;
Speak to my heart, my darling, with thine own
    heart's constant beat;
While I lie on the rock and listen, my love, to thy
    murmurs sweet.

Thou would'st have me sing to thee, heart-loved?
    Alas! I can sing no more;
The songs are gone, and for ever, that I sang thee
    in days of yore,
Ere I knew all the songs of the Ocean, the songs of
    the Hill and Plain;
And can I, knowing their music, sing my puny songs
    again?

Thou hast taught me the songs of the Ocean : for he
    ever sings of thee ;
And all things join in the chorus with the voice of
    the agèd Sea ;
And his full deep music is hallowed with the sound
    of thy name, my sweet,
As he climbs on the rock's hard ledges to kiss my
    darling's feet.

Thou hast taught me the song that the sad wind
    sings in the summer grass :
'Tis to thee ;—and I hear the green trees whisper to
    thee as we pass ;
And the sweet pale flowers scatter their scent in a
    song to thee,
As this rose ;—and see, I have kissed it, if perchance
    it may speak for me.

I heard the voice of a skylark, as I sang at the dawn
    of day,
And I knew that a spirit was singing to wile thy soul
    away ;
And I hushed my song to silence, as I lay on the
    grassy ground,
Lest the spirit should hear me singing, and know
    where my love is found.

Listen, my love, to the singing of birds and wind
    and sea;

Listen, my love, to their singing, and think that they
    sing for me;

For I know that my puny heart-songs would fall
    from my lips in vain,

If I strove, amid the strains of those great ones, to
    sing my songs again.

Waking.

COLD fingers clasped in mine,
  Cold fingers of a friend,—
A friend for aye beloved
  Unto the long world's end.

I dreamed of kisses warm ;
  I could have sworn they passed
'Twixt your hot lips and mine, dear : —
  But I have waked at last :

Have waked to know that pain
  And love-grief have an end :
I died to our old love-life,
  And live again,—thy friend.

Malo Mori.

It is better to die than live, for life is the name of
  sorrow,
And we gather our pleasures to-day, to give them to
  death to-morrow,
And we sit in the shadow, and weep for the joys
  that are lost for ever,
    And the friends that shall come back, never !

It is better to die than live, for death is the end of
  weeping ;
We shall dream as the high God dreams, in his
  everlasting sleeping ;
Our dreams shall be joys and friends, as his is the
  world, for ever ;—
    They shall vanish at waking, never !

Two Sweet Mays.

Thy hair was dark as night, love;
Thy bosom soft and white, love;
And bright thine eyes as light, love;—
         Last sweet May.

Primrose and oxlip bell, dear,
Sweet in the shade-loved dell, dear;
And fell my sin as hell, dear,
         Last sweet May!

The grave is sheer and steep, love;
And hell is dark and deep, love;
'Tis better sleep than weep, love,
         This sweet May.

The world is morning-grey, dear;
But God is good as day, dear:
That He may slay me pray, dear,
         This sweet May.

" Don't You Remember? "

DON'T you remember that sunny day
    (In spring the groves sweet blossoms bear),
We crowned her once with the silver may ?
    Hawthorn boughs for a maid to wear.

Don't you remember that evening, now
    (The summer woods rich odours bear),
Laburnum and lilac upon her brow ?
    Purple and gold for a queen to wear.

Don't you remember another morn,
    (The autumn winds pale dead leaves bear),
When she lost the blossom to find the thorn ?
    Thorns are a crown for sin to wear.

Don't you remember a death of pain
    (The winter storms sad wailings bear),
When the love that was lost was found again ?
    Hawthorn boughs for the pure to wear.

Il Traviato.

Gold in the sun shone the gleaming gorse
   That glowed on the barren strand ;
And gold in the sun shone the hair of a corse,
   As it lay on the white sea-sand.

The lark in the heavens ceased to sing :
   But the curlew shrieked the clearer,
And the raven whirled on his dusky wing,
   And the white gull circled nearer ;

And the full sea moaned with a woman's moan,
   As soft to her breast she drew him :
But the wind in the mountains laughed alone,
   As she laughed alone that slew him.

A Tale of the Rebellion.

IT was the time when summer died,
  And seemed the sweeter as she faded,—
  When evening clouds the valleys shaded,—
I knelt upon the mountain side.

The sun had set ;—one little rim
  Still rose above the waters lowly ;
  I watched the red tip sinking slowly,—
I watched it, waiting there for him.

For he had promised once again
  To meet me there before we parted,
  And I was waiting, broken-hearted,
To see him coming up the glen.

He came,—he leaped the narrow stream ;
  He came,—we spake not long together,
  For, o'er the dry and purple heather,
We saw his comrades pike-heads gleam.

And then I thought his shone more bright,
  And watched it through the glooming weather,
  Till all, across the swelling heather
Slow marching, faded from my sight.

My heart fled from me, kneeling there ;
  But, though my soul was sad and lonely,
  I thought, " I'll pray for Ireland only ; "
And then I breathed a bitter prayer.

I knelt and prayed for victory :
  I prayed—yet scarce my prayer was spoken,—
  That, though my own heart might be broken,
My friends—my people—might be free.

And when the midnight shadows fell
  They found me ;—and I vowed to Heaven
  My heart as sacrifice, that even,
For Ireland, whom I loved so well.

A month had fled, and Autumn rose ;
  The dying leaves were slowly falling,
  And wailing winds were sadly calling
Their loves, the winter storms and snows.

And then, one eve, across the plain,
   And up the mountain's shaggy heather,—
   All blinded by the pelting weather,—
I watched them marching back again.

Their work was o'er ;—the rain-dimmed sun
   Showed joy on all the faces round me;
   But I—alas, my sorrow bound me,
And all who left were there, save one.

God gave them peace; but, even now,
   He whom I loved, and loved him only,
   He bent beneath the gallows lonely ;
And God had listened to my vow.

Sirius.

WHEN sweet-eyed spirits round the windows hover,
   At the first breathing of the gloaming grey,
And the soft shadows of the evening cover
   The sins and sorrows of the dying day;

Then the sad moon, in nightly penance dreary,
   Crosses the pathless desert of the sky,
And hastes, with pallid face and footsteps weary,
   A soul that may not rest and dare not die.

But when she sinks beneath the rim of Ocean,
   And hastens to her home afar from earth,
To hide her silent sorrows in devotion,
   The sweet stars glitter with a fresher mirth.

They look on us with glances true and tender,
   Piercing our spirits with their sleepless eyes;
And one among them shines with tenfold splendour,
   Brighter than all the children of the skies.

O Prince of all the gleaming sons of Heaven!
  O Leader of the glad celestial host!
Thou art to me the dearest joy of even;
  Thou art the friend my spirit longs for most.

I know that thou canst hear me vainly calling,
  In that undying heaven where thou art;
I know that thou canst see my sad tears falling;
  I know that thy keen sight can read my heart.

Wilt thou not speak to me, O child of glory,
  And tell me why my heart so yearns for thee?
I know that thou canst tell me all our story,
  All that we knew ere earth began to be.

Thou wilt not speak! And yet I love thee, spirit,
  More than I love the children of this earth;
And when I shall, in my last days, inherit
  The dim great halls of him who knows no mirth,

Let me be laid where, in the flower-strewn meadows,
  Over my head the long lush grass shall wave,
And do thou come with the soft midnight shadows,
  And look upon me in my silent grave.

E

Three Fragments.

I.

THE CASTLE.

I BUILT a castle upon a steep
  By a stately river's side ;
And black and stormy and broad and deep
  Was that unattempted tide.
And I said to my soul, " For rest and sleep
  Is this ever-silent tower :
  For the wings of darkness with magic power
Brood on the battlements frowning high,
And the turrets are built in the silent sky,
Far from the noise of the earth, and above
All that you fear and hate and love :
And the river, flowing dark and wide,
Shuts you in with its murky tide :
  So nought that you dread can enter here ;

And sound there is none save the wavelets breaking,
Far, far, below; and the night-owl waking,
　When the white moon rises in heaven clear.
　　Then sleep!
For here in life is the peace of the grave."
And my soul looked down on the silent wave
From the castle-top. (From tower to sky,—
From the cliff to the top of the turret high,—
From the wave to the cliff's o'erhanging crest,—
　None of these heights was less or more
Than the depth of the blackening billow's breast,
　And the breadth of the river from shore to shore.)

　My soul was silent and ceased to weep,
For hope and fear were away for ever,
As far from her as sky from river;
　And soon sweet sleep
Hovered above her—a silent spectre,
With a cup of gall and a vase of nectar;
And Joys and Griefs in countless number
Floated around their mistress Slumber.
　　All was vain!—
The cliff and the walls and the turrets steep,
And the iron rocks and the river deep,

To shut out the children of Bliss and Pain,
Who tread in the steps of Thought, or of Sin;
For where Sleep can pass they can enter in.

───

II.

THE ISLAND.

And first they fled to a green-cliffed isle,
   Set like a star in the heaven of Ocean ;
Around it the sea-green wavelets smile,
   And the sea-breeze fans it with placid motion.
No mortal eye hath seen it ever,
And a mortal foot shall tread it never:
For the glamour and spells of the moon surround it,
And by day-time the mists of Ocean bound it,
And the eyes of the mariners who pass
   Are blinded by charms of might ;—they see not
The waves that rise on the gleaming grass,
   And the flowers that in all earth's countries be not.
For every blossom is sweet with scent,
   And every breeze is with perfume laden,
And the sky hangs o'er like an azure tent :
   The unseen isle, like a hiding maiden,

Stands in the midst of its cloudy veil :
None has ever trod it, save spirits pale
Who share in the ever-blessed boon
Of the love of the daughter of the Moon.

III.

THE DEATH OF TYRANNY.

Then they fled away through the silent night,
   Till they saw o'er the waves the lightnings flash,
And the storm-clouds flashing with lurid light,
   And the sound of the awful thunder-crash.
Then my soul was filled with a sudden fear,
For her guide and she were drawing near
   To the midst of the fury and turmoil.
But the moon-maid spake, " Am I not beside thee ?
Nothing of evil shall betide thee :
   It is not for thee that the billows boil ;
Not for thee are the lightnings flashing,
Not for thee is the thunder crashing ;
But heaven and earth are joined in one
To crush the might of a tyrant's throne."

Then they pierced the depths of the stormy cloud,
Through the midst of the thunder pealing loud,
Through the midst of the lightning flashing bright,
And the beating rain of the wintry night.
And they saw that the waves were rushing o'er
A peakèd rock on an iron shore.
The blasts of lightning cleft and tore it,
And the beating rain and storm-wind wore it;
But still it lifted its steely form
Through the frowning heights of the raging storm.
And on its top was a woman bound,
Chained by her hands to the rugged ground.
Around her were beating the blasts of heaven,
And from overhead the planets seven
Seemed to look on her fall and sadness
With rays that told of their joy and gladness:
And eagles, carried upon the storm,
Shrieked and pecked at her prostrate form.
And the songs of the nations filled the air;—
For maidens and stately men were there,
From all the corners of all the world,
'Neath Liberty's lightning-flag unfurled.
They filled the air and they filled the skies,

And sang, " She is conquered now at last !
She has fallen, never more to rise !
Bind her,—ankle, and wrist, and throat,—
  To her lofty rock bind her sure and fast :
She shall never more o'er the dark sea float ;
Never again shall we feel the harm
Of her glance, or the stroke of her mighty arm.
Sorrow and pain shall she send no more
To the hearts and dwellings on every shore.
Let her live unpitied in bitter pain,
And look for a refuge or help in vain ;
As she to us all long since has done,
Be it done to her till the death of the sun ! "
And the moon-maid laughed at the gnawing pains
Of the tyrant that writhed in her iron chains.
My soul was sick at the sight, and strove
  To fly to the help of the panting maid :
  One word in her ear her guardian said,
Which froze up the founts of pity and love ;—
    'Twas the victim's name :
  And she said, " The bliss
  Of revenge like this
    I would buy with a year in burning flame."

King Love.

THE gods, as some old poets sing, dear,
Found out that young Love was a King, dear;
   So they made him a throne of the red, red, gold
   But the chill of the metal hard and cold
Took the blush from his rosy wing, dear.

They vowed that a monarch so great, love,
Should be robed in the mightiest state, lovè;
   So with purple and ermine they wrapped him round,
   But Love cannot live when his wings are bound;
So they found out their error too late, love.

Their gold and their garments were fine, dear,
But they saw that Love could not but pine, dear;
   And though he is King of this rolling ball,
   They found that the very best throne of all
For Love is in your heart and mine, dear.

Cupid Caged.

" O Love, thou hast dwelt in my cottage,
  And nestled all day in my breast ;
Of the sweets of the wood and the meadow
  I spared not to give thee the best.
I brought thee fresh dew of the valley,
  And spoils of the golden-mailed bee,
In the silvery cups of white lilies ;
  But all are untasted by thee."

" Fair maiden, though sweet is the honey,
  And sweet is the dew from the flower,
Yet the food that I live on is sweeter
  Who nestle with thee in thy bower.
I feed on thy rosy lips' kisses,
  Or banquet alone on thy sighs ;
Or I revel from dawning to sunset
  Till drunk with deep draughts from thine eyes."

The Invocation of Venus.

O GODDESS of laughter and sighing,
  Thou giver of pleasure and pain,
Of wisdom that's seasoned with folly,
  Of madness that throbs in the brain ;
Who dwellest in palace and hovel,
  Who rulest in cottage and tower ;—
O'er heroes who charge in the conflict,
  O'er maidens who weep in the bower.
We own thee, the mighty, the awful,
  The Queen of the timid and brave ;
Who burnest the breast of the monarch,
  Who rendest the heart of the slave ;—
We know thee ; we feel thee ; we fear thee ;
  More dread, in thine anger, than fire ;
Oh, visit us not in thy fury !
  Oh, shatter us not in thine ire !

But come to us, gentle and dove-like,—
  And not in thy splendour and might,—
As thou cam'st to the shepherd Anchises,
  All beaming with heavenly light.

When Eris cast into the banquet
  The Hesperidan apple of gold,
Through the midst of the mighty Celestials,
  To the feet of their monarch, it rolled.
He took it, and read, "To the fairest,"
  But dreaded the wrath of his bride;
And a mortal decided the contest
  On Ida's deep-shadowèd side.
So down from their thrones in the Heavens,
  The goddesses swept to the Earth,
From the bridal of golden-haired Thetis,
  From feasting and dancing and mirth.
They came to a glade in the forest
  Of Ida, the mother of trees,
Where the elm and the pine and the cypress
  Are swayed by the murmuring breeze.
And Hera came down in her chariot,
  With the mien and the air of a Queen;
And Pallas, whose cold blue eye glittered
  As bright as the far-flashing sheen

That shone from the joints of her armour,
  In the gleam of the god of the day ;
And she looked, in her helmet, like Ares
  The King of the bloodthirsty fray.
Then Paris, the noble, the god-like,
  Was stricken with awe at the sight;
And the woodland was covered with glory,
  Encircling the goddesses bright.

But when thou didst descend on the mountain,
  The amaranths sprang at thy feet,
And mossroses grew in thy footsteps,
  And lilies and violets sweet :
The primrose and pink were thy carpet,
  And tulips of yellow and red ;
And woodbine entwined with the myrtles
  And cypress, to shelter thy head.
Thy limbs were like ivory polished ;
  Thy bosom, as foam on the rills ;
And thy cheeks as the rose of the sunset
  That shines on the snow-covered hills.
Then Paris, the noble, the god-like,
  Rejoiced in the light of thine eyes,
And he looked not at Pallas or Hera,
  But gave thee, O Venus, the prize.

And thou wert the goddess who bore him
   To Sparta, the land of the free ;
From the fountains of shadowy Ida,
   O'er the waves of the silvery sea :
To fill him with love of fair Helen,
   The beautiful queen of his host ;
Till his city was burned into ashes,
   And honour and glory were lost.

O goddess, thou only art mighty ;
   Thou only art Queen over all,
The beggar who pines in his hovel,
   The noble who feasts in his hall.
Thine are the charms which encircle
   Our hearts with a manacle strong ;—
The charms of soft glances of passion,
   The charms of sweet fragments of song ;
The charms of low murmurs and sighings,
   Of kisses that pierce to the soul—
Black tresses that float on the breezes,
   Bright eyes that can dart and can roll.
Then dwell with us, Venus, we pray thee ;
   Without thee, we live but in vain :
Dispenser of joy and of sorrow,
   And giver of pleasure and pain !

Paris.

LIFT me gently, hero brothers,
  Lay me where my dying eye
May behold the sunny forests
  Where the western breezes sigh.

Let me, once more, see Scamander
  Gilded by the setting Sun ;
Ere he sinks on Ocean's bosom,
  When his daily course is run.

He shall rise again to-morrow,
  Beaming with his wonted light ;
But for me, when day is ended,
  Nought is left but endless night.

Night ! aye, night without a morrow !
  Sleep, from which I ne'er shall wake !
Bring me water, brothers ; water !
  Till my burning thirst I slake.

Where is now Laconian Helen,
  Beaming with her sunny smiles ?
Curses on her radiant glances ;
  Curses on her winning wiles !

Curses on the day I landed
  On the King of Sparta's strand !
Curses on the bark that bore me
  O'er the waves to Hellas' land !

Would that Zeus had, with his lightning,
  Sunk it deep beneath the wave !
Would that 'neath the blue Ægean
  I had found a watery grave !

Or that, on the day my mother—
  Hapless mother !—brought me forth,
Some fire-breathing wind had swept me,
  Scorched and lifeless, from the earth !

" Helen prays to see me, longing
  To behold my face again—"
Sooner would I clasp an adder
  Than endure the stinging pain

And the anguish of her presence,
  Or her voice's hateful tone ;
And her face, though once belovèd,
  Now, to me, has odious grown.

I remember, when Œnone
  Held my head upon her knee ;—
From Mount Ida to the sunset
  None were happier than we !

I was then a simple shepherd ;
  Now, a palace is my home :
Yet I'd rather dwell on Ida
  Than beneath this lofty dome.

Once the sun was shining brightly,
  When I plucked a blushing rose,
Placed it in Œnone's bosom,
  Spake, " E'en thus my passion glows."

Scarcely had she touched the flow'ret
  When there came a gentle breeze,
Blew the light and tender petals
  Far o'er Ida's thousand trees.

"Ah, my Paris" said the maiden,
    "If the rose were not so gay,
Then, perchance, it might have longer
    Bloomed beneath the summer ray;

" Better is the true devotion
    Of the sun-flower to the sun :
He looks down on many others,
    She looks up to only one !

" Thou hast sworn that when Œnone
    Is not dearest to thy soul,
Xanthus, backwards, to his fountains
    Shall his golden waters roll.

" Yet I know that thou wilt leave me,
    And wilt seek a foreign shore ;
But, ere Death has closed thine eyelids,
    Thou shalt see my face once more."

Now the dews of death are rising
    On my forehead pale and cold ;
Soon my body shall be lying
    Lifeless 'neath the yellow mould,

F

And I cannot die in quiet
    Till I see her once again ;
Nought, save her beloved presence,
    Can relieve my burning pain.

Lift me gently, hero brothers,
    Bear me to Œnone's side ;
All my ancient love returning
    Bears me on its rushing tide ;

If I live, that life is only
    Pleasant which my darling shares !
If I die, then Death is welcome,
    If Œnone's life he spares !

Song.

WHITHER away, whither away, golden-armoured Bee?
" Over the fields, over the fields, to a Rose that is
    loved by me ;
For my bosom glows with love of the Rose."
                Happy Bee !

Whither away, whither away, silver-vested Boat?
" Over the waves, over the waves, on the white sea-
    foam I float
In the arms of a kind and loving Wind."
                Happy Boat !

Whither away, whither away, joyous-beating Heart?
" Over the hills, over the hills, till I join and never
    part
With the Maiden sweet whom I long to meet."
                Happy Heart !

Song.

COME away, come away,
From a land where the poor are the children of
    sorrow,
And wearily long for a lingering morrow
    To banish the wrongs of a wretched to-day ;
From a land that is woe to the humble and lowly,
Where joys there are none save in pleasures unholy,
    Come away ! come away !

Come away, come away,
O'er a sea where the soft breeze shall gently blow
    o'er thee,
And Heaven in the blue waves be mirrored before
    thee,
    And warm sunbeams kiss thee the whole of the day :
Where at night on the waters the moonlight is
    beaming
On the silvery bridge o'er the ripples a-gleaming ;
    Come away ! come away !

Come away, come away,
To an island, the hope of the lingering morrow,
Where rest is awaiting the children of sorrow,
 And nought shall be known of the wrongs of
  to-day;
We shall dwell in the flower-woods, humble and
  lowly,
Nor dream of the rich and their pleasures unholy;
 Come away! come away!

The Spirit of Summer.

SPIRIT of the Summer night,
  Wrapped in breezes flower-scented ;
Hovering (when the moon gleams bright
  Like a white-robed queen, blue-tented),
O'er the lightly-rippled stream,
Where thine unseen footsteps gleam
On the silver bridge that leads
Far from earth to dewy meads :
Where the simplest flower that blows
Is far fairer than the rose ;
Where sweet odors from the trees
Hover in each gentle breeze ;
And the humblest song bird there
With the skylark might compare.

Spirit of the Summer night,
  All the placid streams do greet thee ;

And the wavelets, gleaming bright,
  Throb, and rise, and leap to meet thee.
Praying thus, they cry to thee,
" O'er thy bridge of silver, we
Long to flee afar, to rest
In thy land, where all are blest.
Bear us on thy wings sublime,
Bear us, spirit, to that clime."
Spirit of the Summer night,
Bear me to that country bright :
There I would for ever be,
If 'twere but to dwell with thee !

The Spirit of Winter.

SPIRIT of the Winter wild,
  Crowned with rays of flashing lightning ;
Sister of the Summer mild,
  O'er thy path of snow-fields bright'ning,
Hasten to the ice-built dome,
Where the storm-winds have their home :
Glacier-columns stand below ;
And, above, a roof of snow,
Silver-gleaming, flashing bright,
In the dawn of northern light.
Round it flaming circles run,
Painted by the scarlet sun ;
And, amid those circles fair,
Thou, O spirit, dwellest there.

Spirit of the Winter wild,
  All the icy lakes adore thee ;

Flowers, the friends of Summer mild,
   Droop and fall and die, before thee;
For they fear thine icy breath
And thy touch of freezing death,
As thou sweepest slowly past;
After thee, the Northern blast
Blows the dead leaves of the trees
O'er a hundred stormy seas.
Spirit of the Winter wild,
Mother Nature's rudest child,
With thy storm blasts o'er the sea
Bear my sorrows far from me.

𝔇eath.

O LORD, Thou hast given us Life
    And the clinging of heart to heart,
Hate, and the wounds of Strife,—
    Love, with a keener smart,—
Joys that are but for an hour,
    And Grief to cleave us in twain,
And Hope, with a healing power,
    To render us whole again ;—
To purge man's heart from his sorrow,
    And raise him again if he fall ;
To point to a happier morrow ;—
    And we thank Thee, Lord, for them all.

We thank Thee for holy Rest,
    When toils of the day are done ;
For Reason, to choose the best,
    And Sight, to behold the sun :

We thank Thee for Labour meet
  Of hand and of heart and mind ;
For Sleep ;—and the visions sweet
  That follow his feet behind :
For Love, though his eyes are sad,
  And he breathes with a poisoned breath,
And he smites when our hearts are glad ;
  But we thank Thee most for Death.

How sweet, to a love-lorn maiden,
  Is Sleep with its visions bright !
Though her soul is with sorrow laden,
  It rests in the gentle night.
She hears a voice in her ear,
  Ere she wakes again to weep ;
And she sees a form that is dear,
  Unseen, save in blessèd Sleep.
But in that sweet Sleep of all,
  That form shall she ever see,
And that voice on her ears shall fall
  Through ages eternally.

How sweet, when the day is done,
  Is Sleep to the weary brain !

We glory in pleasures unwon,
    And wake but to find them vain.
But in that last soft sweet Sleep
    Countless the joys we shall find ;
How long and how high and how deep !—
    Unknown to an earthly mind.
Faces of lost ones dear
    Shall hover around us again ;
And the bliss that we hoped for here ;—
    Nor waking, to find it vain.

We thank Thee, Lord, for the Joys
    Thou hast given on earth to man ;
Though too fast his pleasure cloys,
    And his days are but a span :
We thank Thee for Love and Strife,
    And the glancing of happy eyes,
For the burning bliss of Life,
    And Reason, that never lies.
We thank Thee for Friends that are dear ;
    We thank Thee for living breath ;
For our Knowledge and Pleasure here ;—
    But we thank Thee most for Death !

Memento et Spera.

WHEN first we met, her step was light,
  As we walked by the sounding sea;
And the white-foamed billows, in sunset bright,
  Re-echoed sweet minstrelsy:
But the sound of her voice was as sweet to me,
And brighter her eyes than the sun-dyed sea.

We met again, and her cheek was pale,
  As we sat by the moaning sea,
Which ever sounded a sad soft wail
  Of mournful minstrelsy:
And still her voice was as sweet to me
As the gentle sound of the silver sea.

We shall meet again; in a lovely land,
  By the shore of a crystal sea,
And hear the strains of a holy band
  Of angel minstrelsy:
And her voice shall again sound as sweet to me
As it sounded of old by the glorious sea.

𝔉riends that are 𝔊one.

Where hast thou borne them, Death,—the friends
    whom we loved and cherished,—
  The eyes that glowed and shone with the light
    and fire of truth ?
Has the health-flush left those cheeks ? Have the
    rippling hair-waves perished,
  That lay like crowns on the brows that beamed
    with the blood of youth ?
Are those sweet voices hushed, that once, when hope
    was high,
Re-echoed with silver laughter in years that have
    gone by ?

Where hast thou borne them, Death ? Mid blos-
    soms with honey laden,
  Do they hear the songs of birds that have not a
    mortal birth ?
Where pleasant trees drop odours on youth and
    on happy maiden,

Do they wander in woodlands fairer far than those
of earth ?

Where weariness sinks into rest ; where pleasures
never cloy :

And the sounds of the summer streams are songs of
ceaseless joy.

Where hast thou borne them, Death ? I hear the
sea-breeze sighing,

Still ;—and the sound of laughter rides on the
wings of the wind,—

Still ;—but another laugh, that is dead and yet undying,

And a still small voice re-echo of days that are
left behind.

From whence are those sweet tones wafted, King of
our souls ? and where

Does that rippling laughter float on the silken summer air ?

Where hast thou borne them, Death ? Thou camest
in robes of glory,

And beauty and brightness shone from the orbs of
thine azure eyes ;

Not as thou comest, with rest, to the head that is
    bent and hoary ;
  Not with the crown of fame that thou makest the
    soldier's prize :
With lovely looks thou did'st lure them out of the
    light of day,
And lead them, with lover's wiles, to thy kingdom far
    away.

Where hast thou borne them, Death ? Oh, speak
    from thy bosom hollow !
  Lift up, at length, the veil that lies on thy brow of
    snow !
Thou hast taken our friends away, O Death, and
    how can we follow ?
  Thou hast taken our friends, and where thou hast
    laid them how can we know ?
Bring them not back to this earth of parting and
    grief again,
But bring us to where they rest, to the land where
    dwells no pain !

Joan of Arc at the Stake.

To the stake!   To the stake!
   The witch to the stake!
Let us hear the winds play 'mid the flames! why
   delay
   To hurry the witch to the stake?
     Bring her forth from the gaol
       To the faggots dire
       And the death of fire:
     Ha! witch, does thy courage fail?

To the stake! to the stake!
Holy pleasure we take
     In the death of the God-hated:
Bring her forth: let her see
To what wage and fee
     Witches are fated.

Mid the roll of drums that mock her, she comes
  In her flashing mail.
   White! were not black more meet
   For the winding sheet
  Of the servant of sin? And upon her brow
 Her helmet gleams in the sun's white beams :
  Witch, doth thy master aid thee now ?
    Does her courage fail ?
    No ;—her cheek is pale,
  But she stands as straight as e'er she stood ;
 And with steadfast eye she looks on high :
   Can a witch pray to God ?
 I know not : perchance 'tis to Satan her master
 She prays to defend her from death and disaster!
 Witch, he hath failed thee at last !
 And we hold thee fast,
Nor can Hell's black bands loose from our hands
   Thee, doomed to the stake !
   To the stake ! to the stake !

  And the helm on her brow !—
  Smite it off! smite it off! and now
   Let us see her shake
    In fear of death.

No, she draws her breath
More calmly than we :
And about her, see
How her golden hair floats on the wind !
Is her beauty from Hell ?   Then Hell is kind :
Agnes Sorel is not so fair,
Her forehead is bare,
Unruffled by fear or sorrow.
What ! doth she not dread the morrow
In flames of Hell ? or earthly fire
To-day ?

What doth the priest say ?
"Wreak ye your ire
In torments of fire
On the victim fated !
'Tis true she is fair :
What need ye care ?
She is not the less hated
By God and man.
Many fairer fell to be servants of Hell !"
Ah ! witch, thy earthly span
Is well-nigh done ;
Thy course is run

Of sin and of Satan's work.
Thou canst not shirk
 The last dread stage of fire; 'tis well
 If thy soul 'scape Hell!

She is bound to the stake;
Those chains will break
Her tender limbs; beware, lest ye take
Their prey from the flames as ye smite her!
Fire the faggots now; the blaze will light her
 Out of the earth.
 And sing; for mirth
Is due when a witch is slain!
We should joy in her pain,
When she feels the rod of an angry God.
 Fire the pile! Fire the pile!
 Let her body vile
 Be consumed in the flame,
 And the witch's name
  Perish for aye!

What is this? The witch would pray!
She is filled with fear for her soul; is a
 crucifix here?

What should she want with the holy rood?
In her hand 'twere useless wood !
   How the soldiers laugh
As she wishes to pray !
The priests keep away,
   For her soul is lost.
See ! a soldier takes
   A walking-staff :
Will he smite her ? No, he breaks
   And binds it with twine,
     And the fragments crossed
   Form the blessèd sign.
There, witch, is a cross for thee !
Pray quickly ; for we
     Will not be delayed :
   We have come to see thee die !

     Her prayer is said.
       Fire the pile ! Fire the pile !
How the flames mount on high !
     For many a mile
The blaze can be seen !
How the torment keen

Of the fiery flame
Thrills through her frame !

To such a doom God-hated
Witches are fated.

Turkey and Serbia.

AN APPEAL TO BOTH HOUSES.

July, 1877.

My Lords and Gentlemen, the East is red
　With blood of battle and with slaughter dire :
On Christian flesh the Turkish hounds are fed ;
　And Christian roofs are prey for Moslem fire ;
And Christian blood like water flows ;—but then,
'Tis not *your* blood, my Lords and Gentlemen !

The Turk is tyrant o'er a hapless land ;
　He wrings the tribute from his helpless slaves ;
They toil for him and for his robber-band ;
　One rest they have,—in their dishonored graves.
Their sons are torn away and slain ;—but then
They're not *your* sons, my Lords and Gentlemen !

And in the eve, when day's sore toil is done,
  The Christian slave has rest from his hard lot :—
But, in the glowing of the setting sun,
  He sees the red flames of his burning cot,
His children slaughtered ;—and his wife—but then
Your wives are safe, my Lords and Gentlemen !

He strikes the tyrant, battling for the right ;
  You watch the conflict safely from afar :
What is it to you which may win the fight ?
  Save that investments totter during war !
You have for birthright what he claims ; and then
You need not care, my Lords and Gentlemen !

My Lords and Gentlemen, I have been told
  That England helped the slave to break his chain,
Giving to aid him both her blood and gold,
  To blot out from the earth a damning stain :
It was not many years ago ; but then
You did not rule, my Lords and Gentlemen !

My Lords and Gentlemen, keep close the sword
  Of help within its gilded shield, and pray
That, when your day of trouble comes, the Lord

May look on you as you look on, to-day,
At his poor servant's dying pangs ;—and then
Sleep with pure souls, my Lords and Gentlemen !

Russia and Poland.

"Vengeance is mine, I will repay:"
saith the Lord.

Is the blood-red sword of Vengeance
　　Sheathed, in the Heavens high ?
Is Truth but an idle fable ?
　　Is Justice but a lie ?
Is God but a madman's raving,
　　The dream of an idiot's brain ?
That you dare to scoff at your sister,
　　When she cries in her bitter pain.

You have taken her diadem falsely,
　　And cast her down from her throne,
And seized on her fertile acres,
　　To add them all to your own ;
Like Ahab, whose own fair vineyards

But widened his wild desires,
Till he murdered righteous Naboth
    For the heritage of his sires.

But there, where the blood of Naboth
    Was poured on the cursèd sod,
His slayer was also stricken
    By the hand of a righteous God !
The guilt of that one red murder
    Drew down the Avenger's sword :
O slayer of thousand-thousands,
    Will you flee from the hand of the Lord ?

No ! though the Lord may linger
    And the feet of His coming be slow,
At last He will raise up the wronged ones
    And lay the usurper low :
For Truth can never be vanquished ;
    And Justice can never lie ;
And the tyrant can never escape it,
    The Vengeance that comes from on high !

The Fontenoy Veteran.

[A veteran of the Irish Brigade, returned to his home on the shore
of Lake Caragh, County Kerry, describes to his grandchildren the
Battle of Fontenoy.]

Yes, Garrett, my armour is dusty;
  My helmet is shorn of its crest;
In its scabbard my good sword is rusty—
  And well has it earned its rest!

Full oft, in the thickest of danger,
  That blade has been flashing, my boy:
It has drunk of the blood of the stranger
  On the field of the great Fontenoy;

When the cry, " Think of beautiful Ireland!"
  Was heard through the midst of the fight,
And we struck down the foes of our sireland;—
  Then, Norah, that corslet was bright.

How gaily Lake Caragh is shining,
  Unrippled by wavelet or breeze !
The beams of the sun-god, declining,
  Are tinting the mountains and trees.

And see how the water is beaming
  With sparkles of green and of white,
And the flashes of red that are gleaming
  On the face of the mirror all bright!

And hark, how from vast Carraun * Tuathill
  The eagles are screaming afar ;
And the Reeks stand, like sons of † MacCumhaile,
  White-crested and panting for war !

Ah ! children, you see but the flashing
  And gleam of the sun on the lake,
Where the ripples round Oulaght are plashing,
  And the tall fir-trees quiver and shake :

But I see again the red battle
  When the Roses were dabbled in gore,

---

    * Pro. " Tuäl."   † Pro. " MacCuäl."

And, through flame and through musketry's rattle,
  The Lily and Shamrock we bore.

    *   *   *   *   *   *

The spring-time the woods was adorning—
  The birds were all singing in joy,
When we rose, at the dawn of the morning,
  In sight of the fair Fontenoy.

And we saw how our foes were advancing ;
  Their red banners shone in the light,
And the glittering sun-beams were glancing
  From helmets and sabres all bright.

And then, how each hero's heart bounded
  'Neath corslet and green-braided vest !
When the notes of the trumpet resounded,
  What passions were stirred in each breast !

Each thought of the green shores of Erin,
  Of mountain, and foam-sparkling lake ;
Of his once happy home ; and the tear in
  His mother's fond eye,—for his sake !

Each thought of the altars forsaken,—
    Of Sassanach sabre and fire ;—
When he heard the drum's rattle awaken
    The depths of his slumbering ire.

We shouted, " For Erin ! " and springing
    To saddle, each drew his bright blade :
The cheer in my ear is still ringing
    That rose from the " Irish Brigade ! "

We charged, like a torrent that, rushing
    From deep mountain-glens to the sea,
Tears down the tall rowan-trees, crushing
    The branches and trunks in its glee.

The Sassanach quailed, and we drove them
    Before us, like dust in the wind ;
And the sky 'gan to thunder above them,—
    The Irish and Death were behind !

The evening star saw us returning
    With laughter and triumph, my boy ;
But deep was the sorrow and mourning
    In England, for red Fontenoy.

Around our gay bivouac sitting,
   That even, we laughed in our glee :
We slept, and the dream-shadows flitting
   Declared that our country was free.

The vision was gone with the morrow ;
   The wrongs of our island remained :
And we woke up again to our sorrow,
   And wept for fair Erin enchained.

But still, we had driven before us
   The British, like chaff in the gale ;
One such battle would surely restore us
   To mountain, and river, and dale,

If we fought with the green banner streaming
   Above us, the green sod below,
And our own sun-burst brilliantly gleaming
   To light our array 'gainst the foe.

*   *   *   *   *   *

Ah! children, my hair has turned hoary;
  The vigour has fled from my hand;
No more, in the fore-front of glory,
  Can I fight for my dear native land.

But look at that lake, and those mountains,
  Our forests and sweet purling rills;
And hark to the roar of the fountains
  That rush down our snowy-capped hills.—

Our mountains, *our* forests, no longer!—
  The land was ours once, to the sea:
In the days when the Right was the stronger,
  In the days when fair Erin was free.

Her sons are the bravest in danger;
  Her daughters, the fairest on earth:
Then, say, should the hand of a stranger
  Still rule o'er the land of our birth?

H

L'Envoi.

A BEAM of the grey light lingered,
　And danced at my darling's feet,
When she stooped in the dale, and lingered
　'Mid violets purple-sweet ;
And my song with the dawn-light lingered
　On the parted lips of my sweet.

The violets faded for ever,
　But faded on her white breast ;
The light of grey dawn for ever
　In her morn-lit eyes found rest :
And my song may be lost for ever
　From the world, if but there it rest.

TRANSLATIONS FROM GREEK POETS.

From the Bacchæ of Euripides.

STROPHE I.

From Asia's plains and Tmolus' sacred hill
I come ; in Bromius' honour I fulfil
     Sweet toil and labour dear,
     While mighty Bacchus I revere.

ANTISTROPHE I.

From road, from house, come out and join our band !
Let every Bacchant pure and holy stand :
     For as the Gods decree
     Shall Dionysus worshipped be.

STROPHE II.

How blest is he who knows the godly rites,
Who leads a pious life, and who delights

His soul with holy dances on the hills,
When pure he stands and washed in sacred rills !
Who honours the orgies of Kybelè grand
With crown of green ivy, and thyrsus in hand,
  And worship due to Bacchus pays !
O Bacchants! O Bacchants! bring Bromius here,
Whom, God and the son of a God, we revere,
  To Hellas' wide and spacious ways !
From Phrygian hills to Grecian homes,
Bacchus himself, the mighty, comes !

ANTISTROPHE II.

Whose mother bore him, ere his destined hour,
Delivered by the wingèd lightning's power ;
His natal day was still with sorrow rife,
The flaming thunderbolt consumed *her* life !
But Zeus him received in his thigh, and concealed
(Lest his birth should to Hêra the proud be revealed)
  With clasps of finely-fashioned gold.
When Fate had ordainèd, he brought him to light,—
The bull-horned God,—and his coronal bright
  Was—snakes in many a gleaming fold !
And thence the Mænads in their hair
The beast-devouring serpents wear.

STROPHE III.

O Thebans, the nurses of Semelè fair,
The garlands of ivy entwine in your hair :
  Abound in the yew with its berries all bright,
    And make yourselves Bacchants with oak and
      with pine,
  And sew on your garments of fawn-skin so light,
    The bunches of wool, and locks snowy and fine :
And consecrate around the saucy wands :
The whole earth soon shall join our joyous bands !
    When Bacchus the orgies shall lead,
      Away ! to the hill ! to the hill !
    At his bidding a crowd of fair women attend,
      Removed from the shuttle and loom at his
      will.

ANTISTROPHE III.

O chamber of darkness in hallowed Krete !
Where Zeus had his dwelling—the Kurêtês' seat !
  Whose triple-plumed priests once invented for me
    The circlet of leather which sounds in my hand :
They mingled their shouts with the happy and free,
    And musical pipes of the Phrygian band.

To Rhea then they gave the leathern round,
With Bacchic cries and revels soon to sound.
    The Satyrs, insane in their joy,
        Obtained it from her by request ;
    Its sounds in their revels triennial inspire
        Deep pleasure and joy in our Bacchus's
        breast!

EPODOS.

When, on the lofty mountain's brow,
The Bacchant flings to earth, ah, how,
   How mighty is his joy !
From bands of revellers he springs ;
In sacred fawn-skin clad, he sings
   His bliss without alloy :
His pleasure is the slaughtered he-goat's blood,
Whose flesh, uncooked and bleeding, is his food :
From Phrygian, Lydian, shores he crossed the sea :—
Great Bromius our leader is :—Evœ !
    The plain, beneath the mountains,
      Is spread, a milky sea ;
    With wine are filled its fountains,
      And nectar of the bee ;
    Like a Syrian censer's fume.

The Bacchant whirls a torch of pine :
Upon his thyrsus see it shine !
Room for the Bacchant ! Room !
He directs the wandering dance,
Raging in a frenzied trance,
And shaking his beautiful hair to the wind :—
Such songs with his music and shouts are combined :
" Come, Bacchanals, come ! the delight of the
    land
Of Tmolus, the mount of gold, solemn and grand !
In praise of your God let the rattling drums sound :
With Phrygian shouts wake the forests around !
Evœ ! to the God who delights in Evœ !
When sweetly the lotos, that hallowèd tree,
Its music harmonious and sacred distils,
With the Bacchants away ! to the hills ! to the
    hills ! "
As a colt with its dam rushes wild o'er the lea
The Mænads exult in their Bacchanal glee.

From the Hecuba of Euripides.

Choral Ode (αὖρα, ποντιάς αὖρα).

STROPHE I.

BREEZE of the ocean, breeze of the sea,
  That bearest afar o'er the briny foam
The ships that swift on their white wings flee,
  Where is the wretched home
That e'en now waits o'er the swelling wave
      For me—a slave?
    Is it in the Dorian land?
    Or where, on Phthia's strand,
The fields with the richest of plenty glow,
  And Apidanus' river-children flow?

ANTISTROPHE I.

Or shall I fly with sea-sweeping oar
  To one of the isles in the far-off sea,
Where palm-trees tall, ne'er seen before,

And laurel, sacred tree,
O'er Leto fair their branches spread
On her child-birth bed ?
Shall I dwell in those sad shades ?
Or, with the Delian maids,
Shall I hymn the bow of Artemis fair
And the golden fillet that binds her hair ?

STROPHE II.

Or, in the city where Pallas rules,
In fair-throned Athena's saffron cloak,
With subtle working of mingled threads
Shall I the steeds to the chariot yoke ?
Or shall I picture the Titan brood,
Whom the Son of Kronos lulls to sleep,
To slumber long and slumber deep,
With his fire that burns the blood ?

ANTISTROPHE II.

Woe to our children ! And woe, our sires !
And woe to the land that gave us birth !
Captive, enslaved by Argive spears,
And smitten, in clouds of smoke, to earth !

But I must dwell by a foreign sea,
    And, a captive, cross the ocean wave ;
    For Asia now is Europe's slave :—
Or Death shall my bridegroom be !

From Moschus.

"The Epitaph of Bion."

SING, springs, a dirge ; lament, O Dorian wave ;
Ye rivers, weep o'er lovely Bion's grave :
Join in our sorrow, every tree and leaf ;
Ye blossoms, bow your clustered heads in grief ;
And you, red roses, and anemones,
Weep for the lord of rustic melodies :
In the sad strain unite, O flower blood-red,
Fair hyacinth ;—the tuneful youth is dead !

Maids in the hills of Sicily who reign,—
Song-loving Muses,—raise the mournful strain !
Ye nightingales, who, 'mid the thick leaves sing,
Among the glens by Arethusa's spring,
Tell all your fellow-birds that he is dead,—
The sweet-voiced herdsman,—and with him has
    fled

The soul of music ; and the Dorian strain
Is lost, for Bion cannot sing again !

Maids in the hills of Sicily who reign,—
Song-loving Muses,—raise the mournful strain !
Swans, whose white plumage Strymon ever laves,
Sing your sad dirges, sailing o'er the waves,
Such as ye sing when your own death is nigh.
Let all the Œgrian damsels hear your cry !
The Dorian Orpheus from the earth has fled !—
Tell the Bistonian nymphs that he is dead !

Maids in the hills of Sicily who reign,—
Song-loving Muses,—raise the mournful strain !
The darling of the herd shall sing no more !
Beneath the lonely oaks, in days of yore,
He sat and sang ; but now his only strains
Are songs of death where gloomy Pluto reigns.
Upon the ancient mountains silence falls :
No soft-eyed cow to her strong comrade calls ;
They wander, without feeding, o'er the plain,
And their soft lowings mourn the gentle swain.

Maids in the hills of Sicily who reign,—
Song-loving Muses,—raise the mournful strain !

Apollo, and the black-cloaked Priâpi,
And Satyrs, wept that thou so young should'st die,
O Bion : and the Pans for the song sighed ;
And the sweet fountains at their sources dried,
Weeping for thee.   Among the rocks of yore
Fair Echo cried ;—but she will cry no more,
Since she no longer can re-echo thee.
And, at thy death, the fruit fell from the tree,
And every blossom faded, and the sheep
Would give no milk, nor would the hive-bees keep
Their sweet honey ;—why should they store it,
        when
Thou can'st not come to gather it again ?

Maids in the hills of Sicily who reign,—
Song-loving Muses,—raise the mournful strain !
The dolphin never grieved in days of yore
Among the morning waves ;—never before
With so much sorrow did the nightingale
Sing on the rocks ;—nor the sad swallow wail
On the tall mountains ;—nor, upon the sea,
Did the gull shriek, weeping Alcyone ;—
Never before did the white waves so ring
With the sad sea-mew's shriek ;— nor did the wing

Of Memnon's bird so often beat around
The hero's tomb, at the first morning-sound,
Mourning the rosy-fingered Dawning's son,
Bion, as now they mourn that thou art gone!

Maids in the hills of Sicily who reign,—
Song-loving Muses,—raise the mournful strain!
The nightingales and swallows (whom he pleased
And whom he taught to sing) the branches seized,
And sang a sad and sweetly-sounding strain,
Responding to each other's cries;—again
The other birds took up the plaintive sound;
And, grieving, you, O ring-doves, cooed around!

Maids in the hills of Sicily who reign,—
Song-loving Muses,—raise the mournful strain!
O well-belovèd, who shall touch the flute
That thy mouth kissed, since those sweet lips are
      mute?
Who is so bold? Thy breath still fills the reeds;
On thy sweet songs, within, sad Echo feeds.
To Pan I bear it:—he can play:—in dread
Lest thou shoulds't vanquish him, although thou'rt
      dead!

Maids in the hills of Sicily who reign,—
Song-loving Muses,—raise the mournful strain !
And Galatea weeps, who once loved thee,
And with thee sat beside the tossing sea.
Thy song was sweeter than the Cyclop's lay,
So lovely Galatea fled away
From him, and looked on thee with eyes of love ;
And now, forgetful of the waves, above
The sandy beach she sits on the high rocks,
And ever watches o'er thy scattering flocks.

Maids in the hills of Sicily who reign,—
Song-loving Muses,—raise the mournful strain !
With thee must die the gifts the Muses gave ;
Maidens' sweet kisses cease within the grave :
Around thy tomb the Loves in sorrow weep,
And Cypris loves thee with a love more deep
Than that she lavished on the gentle boy,
Adonis, at whose death died all her joy.

Maids in the hills of Sicily who reign,—
Song-loving Muses,—raise the mournful strain !
Clear-sounding stream, this is thy second grief !
Another woe, black river ! First, the chief

Of all thy children, Homer died (and he
Was cherished by the Muse Calliope).
'Tis said that all thy countless streams did weep,
And that thy bitter wailings filled the deep :
And now thou mournest for a second son,
Sharing-the grief of many an other one !
Both, of thy streams—of Helicon the first
Drank ;—Arethusa quenched the other's thirst.
One sang of Tyndarus' thrice-lovely child ;—
And Thetis' son, and of his anger wild,
And Menelaus, and his wretched reign :
The other sang not war, or grief and pain,
But Pan he hymned, and pleased the shepherds
    all ;
And with a song he graced both herd and stall ;
He milked a heifer ;—played upon the pipe ;
Taught love to those who were for loving ripe ;
The son of Cypris cherished in his breast ;
And left to Aphrodite all the rest.

Maids in the hills of Sicily who reign,—
Song-loving Muses,—raise the mournful strain !
In all the cities shall thy dirges be ;
More than for Hesiod Askra weeps for thee :

The Theban woods thee, more than Pindar,
    bless;
And lovely Lesbos mourns Alcæus less.
Less for Archilochus fair Paros grieves
Than thee ; and noble Mitylenè leaves
Her grief for Sappho to lament for thee ;
And all in whom the poets' spirits be
Mourn because Bion thus untimely sleeps :
Sicelides, the Samian glory, weeps ;
And he, whose smiling eyes were fair to see,
Cydonian Lycidas, laments for thee :
Among the men who dwell by Halys' wave,
Philetas weaves a garland for thy grave ;
In Syracuse, Theocritus ; and I
Mid the Ausonians raise thy funeral cry.
No stranger am I to the rustic flute ;
I learned from Bion : now his voice is mute,
And I am left to sing the Dorian strain
In place of him who ne'er shall sing again !
To others, master, thou didst leave thy gold :
To me, the song I learned from thee of old !

Maids in the hills of Sicily who reign, —
Song-loving Muses,—raise the mournful strain !

When mallows perish in the garden's shade,
And green parsley and curling anise fade,
They live again at close of winter drear;—
They live and flourish for another year.
But we, the great and strong, the prudent, die
But once; and then in hollow earth we lie,
And, unawakened from our slumber deep,
We sleep a long, a never-ending, sleep.
But not wrapped up in silence dost thou lie;
The nymphs have sent the frog to sing close by:
I do not envy this last minstrelsy,
For his sad song is no-wise sweet to me.

Maids in the hills of Sicily who reign,—
Song-loving Muses,—raise the mournful strain!
Didst thou drink poison, Bion? Could it meet
Such lips as thine, and not turn pure and sweet?
Who mixed or gave to thee a draught so strong,
When thou wert speaking? Since it 'scaped thy
      song.

Maids in the hills of Sicily who reign,—
Song-loving Muses,—raise the mournful strain!
Just is the end of all men here below!—
But I am weeping in my bitter woe,

For Bion's death ; and if it might but be
That I, like Orpheus, could undying see
The depths of Hell,—or like Alcides, sent
In days of old, or as Ulysses went ;—
I too would enter gloomy Pluto's door,
That I might see fair Bion's face once more ;
And if he sings for the dread King of Hell.
That I might hear his sweetest song as well.
Do thou for Cora sing some herdsman's strains,
Some pleasant song of Sicily's fair plains :
She knows the sunny slopes of Ætna well,
Where she has often danced ; and she can tell
The Dorian song ;—nor will thy music be
Slighted by her,—but as Eurydice
Was given back to dwell with living men,
So thou, O Bion, wilt return again !
And, oh, if I could play the lyre as well
As Orpheus, I, for thee, would play in Hell.

THE END.

www.ingramcontent.com/pod-product-compliance
Lightning Source LLC
Chambersburg PA
CBHW020756020726
47495CB00008B/2450